Shimmer and Shine
All Bottled Up!

W9-AWY-679

By **Mary Tillworth**
Illustrated by **Mattia Francesco Laviosa**

Based on the teleplay "**All Bottled Up**" by **Scott Gray**

A Random House PICTUREBACK® Book

Random House 🏠 New York

© 2017 Viacom International Inc. All rights reserved. Published in the United States by Random House Children's Books, a division of Penguin Random House LLC, 1745 Broadway, New York, NY 10019, and in Canada by Penguin Random House Canada Limited, Toronto. Pictureback, Random House, and the Random House colophon are registered trademarks of Penguin Random House LLC. Nickelodeon, Shimmer and Shine, and all related titles, logos, and characters are trademarks of Viacom International Inc.
randomhousekids.com
ISBN 978-1-5247-1718-6
MANUFACTURED IN CHINA
10 9 8 7 6 5 4 3 2 1

Glitter effect and production: Red Bird Publishing Ltd., U.K.

One morning, Shimmer, Shine, and Leah were visiting the Zahramay Falls market. They were shopping for the perfect bottle!

Leah picked one up. "What's in it? Perfume?" She removed the stopper, and glittering fireworks flew out!

Shimmer giggled. "They're magic bottles! Fun things happen when you open them."

Shine opened another bottle, and it started bouncing. It bounced through the streets and onto the sorceress Zeta's head. Zeta glared at the girls.

"Oh, I wish I could catch that bouncing bottle!" Leah exclaimed.

"Boom, Zahramay! First wish of the day!" Shine spun her magic bracelets, and the bottle flew into Leah's hands.

Meanwhile, Zeta wanted to become the most powerful person in Zahramay Falls, so she hatched a plan. The sneaky sorceress conjured up a bejeweled bottle.

"I'll enchant this bottle so that when it opens, it traps those genies," she said. "Then I'll keep the bottle *and* their wishing magic!"

Shine picked up Zeta's bottle. "I wonder what this bottle does."

"Ooooh, it's my favorite color!" Shimmer said, and she pulled out the stopper.

The bottle flew into the air. A huge whirlwind spun out of it, and the genies were sucked inside!

"Are you guys okay?" Leah called into the opening.

"We're fine! But I don't like this bottle enough to live in it," Shimmer said.

"Get us out!" shouted Shine.

Leah knew how to rescue her genies. "I wish Shimmer and Shine were out of this bottle!"

Shine clapped her hands. *"Boom, Zahramay! Second wish of the day! Shimmer and Shine, out of this bottle divine!"*

Magical sparkles zinged around inside the bottle.

"Oh, no!" cried Leah. "The wish magic is trapped inside, too!"

The magic sparkles were so powerful that they shook the enchanted bottle right out of Leah's hands! The bottle rolled onto a flying carpet. When it took off, Leah, Tala, and Nahal hopped aboard Shimmer and Shine's flying carpet, and the chase was on!

"Whoa!" Leah shouted as the carpet zipped through the air. She turned to the pets. "You guys know how to steer this thing, right?"

Tala and Nahal just yowled.

Leah was closing in on the enchanted bottle when Zeta and Nazboo appeared on Zeta's flying scooter.

"We have to make sure those genies and their magic stay all bottled up," cackled Zeta.

"Zeta!" cried Leah. "That tricky sorceress must have done this to Shimmer and Shine."

Zeta and Nazboo caught up to the flying carpet. Nazboo reached out to grab the enchanted bottle.

But Leah zoomed in front of Nazboo. "Not so fast!"
Nazboo leapt back—right onto Zeta's head! The sorceress lost control of her scooter.

"Go, Leah!" shouted the genies.

But their happy cheering made the bottle slip off the carpet and plop into the river below!

Zeta looked up and saw Leah racing toward the enchanted bottle.

"Leah's going to get to the genies first," she said. "Unless I use a potion."

Zeta conjured up a potion that filled the river with bottles that were identical to the enchanted one holding Shimmer and Shine!

With so many bottles in the water, Leah couldn't find the one bottle with her genies! Shine had an idea. "Shimmer! Shimmer more than you've ever shimmered before!" Shimmer grinned. "And Shine, shine on!"

Light sparkled from their enchanted bottle.

Leah saw the light and flew the carpet down to them.

Zeta and Nazboo sped toward the bottle, too. Nazboo leaned over the edge of their scooter and swiped at it. He missed!

A split second later, Tala grabbed the bottle out of the water!

Once they all were safe on dry land, Leah had an idea. "Maybe if I rub the bottle like I rub my genie necklace, you'll come out," she said. She rubbed—and out flew Shimmer and Shine!

"You saved us, Leah!" shouted Shimmer.

Leah laughed and ran to the genies. Even without all her wishes, the day had turned out great!